With all my love to Rebekah, Eric, and Oliver
— D.H.

For Helen, Reverend LaVerne, Sharon, and the Sasaki family,
who've inspired me to live a mindful life
— S.N.-B.

Sounds True
Boulder, CO 80306

Text © 2020 by Deborah Hopkinson
Illustrations © 2020 by Shirley Ng-Benitez

Published 2020

Book design by Ranée Kahler

Printed in South Korea

Library of Congress Cataloging-in-Publication Data

Names: Hopkinson, Deborah, author. | Ng-Benitez, Shirley, illustrator.
Title: Mindful day / by Deborah Hopkinson; illustrations by Shirley
    Ng-Benitez.
Description: Boulder, CO : Sounds True, 2020. | Summary: Illustrations and
    easy-to-read text observe a young girl as she and her family practice
    mindfulness through a busy Saturday.
Identifiers: LCCN 2019014673 (print) | LCCN 2019017673 (ebook) |
    ISBN 9781683643227 (ebook) | ISBN 9781683642794 (hardback)
Subjects: | CYAC: Mindfulness (Psychology)—Fiction. | Family life—Fiction.
Classification: LCC PZ7.H778125 (ebook) | LCC PZ7.H778125 Min 2020 (print) |
    DDC [E]—dc23
LC record available at https://lccn.loc.gov/2019014673

10 9 8 7 6 5 4 3 2 1

Mindful Day

by Deborah Hopkinson

Illustrated by Shirley Ng-Benitez

It's still dark
when one small bird
fluffs his feathers
and lifts his voice
to sing up the sun.

Snuggled deep in our dreams,
we hear his clear song.
And we open our eyes
to the gift of a new day.
This day.
Our day.

Together we breathe:
in out,
soft slow.
I look
and listen.
I smile.

The world stirs.
A car honks, a door slams,
a bus rumbles by.
A tiny dog trots
yap, yap, yapping
down the street.

"Feed me," the kitten begs.
Baby cries for his breakfast, too.
Little ones have a hard time waiting, don't they?
Good morning, baby.
Good morning, family.

We place spoons and bowls,
shake out some cereal—*shake, shake*—
and sprinkle bright berries on top.
I pop one in my mouth and close my eyes.
I chew slowly. It tastes sweet as summer.

We take our time getting ready:
shirt, pants, socks, shoes.
One, two, three, four.
Can't find a shoe?
That's ok, we'll look together.

Brush teeth and hair,
pick up toys,
and make the bed.
We pay attention
to each simple task.

Together we breathe:
in out,
soft slow.
I look
and listen.
I play.

At first, the sun is out
to warm us on our walk.

We get fruit at the Saturday market,
a hummingbird feeder at the store,
an armful of library books.

Find one for baby, too.
It's fun to make him laugh.

On the way home,
the billowing clouds
burst into a shower.
Hard rain drums the leaves
and patters our hands and heads.
Baby cries out in surprise.
Babies have a hard time being wet, don't they?
It's all right, baby!
We'll be home soon.

Together we breathe:
in out,
soft slow.
I look
and listen.
I run!

Thunder crashes.
Rain spatters the
windowpane.
How lucky we are
to have a snug roof,
to be safe and loved.

After nap and play,
it's time to cook dinner:
chop veggies,
make a salad,
boil potatoes.
Yum! Bright crunchy carrots.
Fresh crispy lettuce.

Everyone can help—
even baby (well, sort of).

In the flickering candlelight,
we hold hands
before we begin.
"We are thankful for this meal,
the work of many people, and
the sharing of food from the
earth and sea."

Together we breathe:
in out,
soft slow.
I look
and listen.
I eat.

Bath time,
book time,
bedtime.
Hush, baby!
Goodnight, kitten!
Our day is almost done.

At just this moment,
a big silver moon
peeks out from behind a cloud
to light up the night.

Now we gaze at it
and breathe together:
in out,
soft slow.
One last hug
before I sleep.